WELCOME TO LOON LAKE

A STRAYS OF LOON LAKE ROMANTIC COMEDY SHORT STORY

KITTY BUCHOLTZ

Daydreamer
Entertainment

Welcome to Loon Lake

Published by Daydreamer Entertainment

Copyright © 2012, 2016 by Kathleen Bucholtz

ISBN: 978-1-937719-13-5
ISBN: 978-1-937719-12-8 (ebook)

Cover Design: John Bucholtz
Cover photo © Deklofenak — DepositPhotos.com

Edited by Marcy Weydemuller

For my Sydney writers group —
Ann, Bernadette, Coleen, Deb, Jen, Judy, Margie, Paula,
and Shaz

Your infectious enthusiasm for celebrating every writing
achievement is unmatched...and sorely missed!
I love you guys!

Welcome
to Loon Lake

Kitty Bucholtz

WELCOME TO LOON LAKE

*L*ena Hart adjusted a knob on her new telescope. *Perfect.* The moon filled the viewfinder. Mostly. Tonight a partial lunar eclipse would decorate the night sky and Lena was determined to see it. She'd lived her whole life in the city of Lansing or the nearby suburbs, and rarely saw the stars in all their glory. Now that she'd moved to the country, she wanted to experience everything city life couldn't offer.

Already a big chunk of the moon appeared to be missing, like a bite had been taken out by a giant space monster. Lena leaned back in her camp chair and gazed at the rest of the Michigan sky. So many stars. More than she'd ever seen before.

She peeked into the tent in her new backyard. Her five-year-old, Joey, slept like the dead. She'd have to tell him about her giant space monster theory in the morning. She knew he watched too many movies. Perhaps a better mom would insist that her son find more intellectually stimulating ways to spend his time, but the fact was that they both enjoyed a good monster movie. Though Joey's were usually animated.

A memory rushed in — cuddling in her husband Tim's arms on the couch as they watched the entire *Godzilla* boxset on New Year's Day. A Hart family tradition they'd started when they were dating. They groaned together at the cheesy bits, laughed at the dialogue, and discussed the evolution of special effects.

Joey loved the *Godzilla* cartoons and watched them on Saturday mornings, but Lena hadn't seen a *Godzilla* movie since Tim died two years ago. She took a deep breath and let her eyes focus again on the sky. The pain had dissolved over time to a dull ache, but sometimes it would stab her unexpectedly, like pain from a phantom limb.

Looking back at the moon, she tried to lighten her mood. She imagined a monster with 2-D vision seeing the moon as a giant white chocolate and macadamia nut cookie. He'd take a little bite first. Yum. One more bite. Good stuff. Then he'd settle invisibly in the sky and eat the moon one bite at a time, leaving Earth's astrologers to think it was just another lunar eclipse. Until they realized the moon wasn't coming back. The earth's tides would shift, massive tsunamis would wipe out Los Angeles and New York and—

Something moved in the woods at the edge of the yard. Something big.

Lena's hands tightened on the arms of her camp chair. She listened for another sound, leaning forward to peer into the trees. Why, oh why, was she thinking about monsters when she'd just moved to the country? They weren't quite as funny when faced alone in the dark.

She picked up a flashlight and pointed it toward the woods. Nothing. No squirrels or rabbits or raccoons. Not even a tree branch moved.

Maybe it was her imagination.

Country life would take some getting used to. The worst kind of critters in the city were raccoons, if you didn't count

Lansing's politicians. Lena wasn't sure what kinds of animals roamed Loon Lake. Surely bears lived much deeper in the woods. Did bobcats come out at night? Deer didn't make that much noise, did they? As the quiet continued, her fears ebbed away. Moving here was a good idea. Getting away from the life she'd had with Tim would help her to heal more completely. That's what she was counting on anyway. She could live with her loneliness, but she was beginning to worry about her son growing up without a father. She felt she owed it to Tim as well as Joey to do the best she could for Joey, no matter the cost. But she couldn't go on dates in the same city where she'd gone on dates with Tim. She couldn't build a new life over the ruins of the life she'd loved.

Lena took another calming deep breath and it turned into a yawn. She looked forward to starting her new job as a first grade teacher at Loon Lake Elementary in a couple weeks, where Joey would start kindergarten. The two of them were ridiculously excited. They had new bags, new school supplies, new clothes...and a new bounce in their steps.

Lena glanced toward the quiet woods at one side of the rental house. No matter what they had to get used to, the changes were for the good.

As the giant space monster ate away at the moon, Lena got sleepier. When all that could be seen was the white outer edge, she sighed and smiled. Perfect. Now she could check "see lunar eclipse" off her list of new adventures.

She dropped into her sleeping bag, curled up next to her son, and fell asleep.

She dreamed of cookie monsters from outer space coming down to have dinner with her and Joey. The cookie monsters had horrible manners, ripping plastic and chewing noisily with their mouths open.

Lena awoke with a start. She opened her eyes in the early

morning light and came face to face with a little black bear. She rubbed her eyes and looked again. The bear was halfway across the yard, running for the woods. But running like a—

It wasn't a bear, it was a dog.

She pulled herself out of her sleeping bag. The ground outside the tent was littered with the remains of their hot dog dinner. Two hot dogs were left in the ripped-open package. *Great.* Neighbors who let their dogs roam free.

She glanced toward the woods. At the edge, the animal stared back at her, poised to run away. Maybe it was looking at her, or maybe it was more interested in the hot dogs in her hand. The hand holding the meat fell to her side. The dog tracked the movement.

"Poor guy," she murmured. "Homeless and hungry? Here I thought I'd left the homeless behind in the city."

She shouldn't. She really shouldn't. It would only encourage him to come back, raid her trashcans, perhaps bring fleas and who knows what into her yard.

Lena knelt down and pulled a hot dog out of the package.

The dog lowered his head and stared.

She held it out. "Here, boy, come on. You can have it."

A full minute went by before the dog took a couple steps toward her. He stopped. The animal was covered in mud and debris. No wonder she'd thought he was a bear.

Lena waited. She broke off a third of the meat and showed it to him. She tossed the piece so that it landed about ten feet from his nose. He took a couple steps back, looked at the meat, looked at her, sniffed the air, and trotted over. He gobbled it up in one bite and raised his head to Lena.

She smiled. "Good dog. Good boy." She leaned slowly toward the tent, careful not to scare the dog but not wanting her son to miss this. "Joey. Joey! Wake up, baby. I want to show you something."

Some mumbling and shuffling sounds came from inside. Then the cutest little blonde boy — not that she was biased —

crawled out of the tent on his hands and knees. She held her finger to her lips and pointed. His sleepy blue eyes got bigger when he saw the dog.

"My dog!" he said. He crawled over and leaned up against Lena. "The one I asked God for."

Lena glanced down at him. "What? I don't know whose dog it is, honey, but I'm sure he belongs to someone. I don't think God sent him." She looked at the messy coat and noticed how thin the dog looked. What was he covered in? Mud and wood chips? For heaven's sake, where had he been? Maybe he didn't have an owner.

The dog stared at them, his tail making the faintest wagging motion. Maybe he'd had a family with small children. He seemed to want to come over and be friendly. The thought crossed her mind that maybe God *had* sent them a dog. Or maybe the animal was still focused on the hot dog, not on finding a new family.

Lena pulled off another piece and tossed it to him. He gobbled it up and took another few steps in their direction. She threw another piece so that he'd have to come closer. Under the mud she could see what might be black and white fur. He looked like a mutt to her, at least with the mud. Mutts were supposed to make good pets, right? Loyal and smart and gentle. That's what she'd heard anyway.

"Look, Mom," Joey pointed. "He has one blue eye and one brown eye. That's so *weird*."

She tossed the dog another piece of meat. He caught it in the air.

Joey laughed. "Let me, Mom!" He reached for the last hot dog.

"Okay, hold on, hold on." Lena broke off a piece and handed it to her son. He tossed it into the air and the dog jumped to get it. Joey threw him another piece, and another. The tail was definitely wagging now. Muddy ears perked up after he ate the last piece.

"Excuse me, ma'am." A man's voice came from behind the tent. "Please back away from the animal."

CW Emerson kept his voice neutral, his body stance neutral. *Don't scare the dog.* CW glanced at the little boy. *Don't scare the boy.* He didn't want the kid to grow up scared of dogs, and this animal looked half wild and hungry.

The dog dropped his head as he watched CW. His tail stopped wagging. *Aw, great.* CW loved dogs. He hated for them to see him as the enemy. He wondered if there was something inherent in his Animal Control uniform that clued the animals in.

The woman was staring at him but not minding what he said. "Ma'am," he put a bit more steel in his voice. "Please take your son inside until I take care of the dog."

"What are you going to do to my dog?" The little boy jumped to his feet.

CW blinked. *His* dog?

"It's okay, Joey," the woman said. Her voice had a soothing tone. CW liked it. "Go inside and I'll take care of, uh —" She looked at the dog. "Chip."

CW chuckled inside. He'd bet his truck that dog didn't have a name a minute ago. Did the woman think he was born yesterday? "I'm taking him to the animal shelter. If you want to come down and fill out the appropriate paperwork, you can—"

"No! He's mine!" the boy yelled. He grabbed his mother's hand but kept his eyes on CW.

He kept his voice calm. "I won't hurt him," CW said.

The boy stared at him, weighing whether CW could be trusted. After a moment, he nodded and opened the patio's sliding glass door. Inside, he peered out, his hands and nose pressed against the glass.

Well, no pressure now.

"I'm sorry, who are you?" The woman raised her eyebrows but not her voice. CW had the sensation he was back at school, caught by the teacher for some unknown infraction.

"CW Emerson, ma'am. I'm with Animal Control. Your neighbor called," he pointed vaguely over his shoulder, "and said there was a wild animal running loose."

CW took in the tent, the telescope, and the tiny outdoor grill. He hadn't camped in the back yard since — he couldn't remember. Junior high, maybe? Looking over the scene, he had the urge to do it again. He wondered if they'd had s'mores last night. He walked a few steps closer and watched the dog. No growling, but no tail wagging.

"I'm sorry you were bothered, Mr. Emerson, but my dog —" Did she choke on the words? "—got away from me, that's all. He's not wild." She glanced toward the house.

The kid watched them from inside, his face scrunched up with worry until he met CW's gaze. Then he smiled a little and gave a small wave. CW sighed and tried to smile back. The trust of a child was a heavy burden to carry. He didn't know if he was up to it today.

He looked back at the woman still kneeling on the ground. She, on the other hand, didn't seem to trust him one bit. Plus, she was obviously lying, stuttering every time she made up something on the spot. And she seemed oblivious to how bad a liar she was.

"Well, Ms.—?"

"Hart. Lena Hart. I just moved here." She moved slowly to her feet, watching the dog. Then she turned to him and stuck out her hand. "Nice to meet you."

CW noticed the leaf in her hair as he shook her hand. It was probably more polite to ignore it, but he reached out and pulled the leaf away. Her dark springy curls bounced a bit as she moved her head aside. He showed her the leaf and dropped it to the ground.

She blushed.

CW glanced toward the house. Did married women blush? But even if she were single, this wasn't the time or the place. Too bad. She was a striking-looking woman. He cleared his throat and checked out the dog again. He'd come a few steps closer.

"Could you call your dog, please, Ms. Hart?" Professionalism. That's what he needed to remember.

She paused, then put on a smile as sunny as the summer morning. "Sure," she said with unnecessary joviality. At least she hadn't stuttered. She turned her back to him and bent over with her hand out. CW let his gaze wander downward for a moment. Nice.

He reminded himself he was on the clock. He folded his arms and assumed the air of a pseudo-government employee, one part boredom to two parts detachment.

"Here, Chip," she called. "Here, boy." Lena Hart — her name inspired a certain sexiness that was currently underscored by her body — looked over her shoulder at CW. He raised his eyebrows innocently at her, but something in his expression must've given him away. She jerked upright and blushed some more. CW grinned after she turned away. Two parts sexy to one part adorable.

Lena squatted down and snapped her fingers. "Come on, Chip." She sounded annoyed. The dog sat down and tilted his head at her. She kept calling. The dog yawned. Lena looked at the empty hot dog wrapper in her hand. When it rustled, the dog jumped to his feet, looking expectant.

CW followed her gaze around the campsite. Hot dog buns, half eaten by the dog. An unmolested box of graham crackers. A cooler. Lena opened the cooler and pulled out a Hershey bar.

The dog moved a few feet closer, wagging his tail.

CW couldn't stand there and let her poison the dog. "You're not going to feed that to him, are you?" He watched as she hesitated, confused. "Since chocolate is poisonous to dogs." He raised his eyebrows at her.

"Of course not." She frowned at him. "I haven't had breakfast." She pulled off the top of the wrapper and took a bite.

It was all CW could do not to laugh. This was the most fun pick-up he'd had in months.

"Want one?" As if to prove that she never intended to feed the candy to the dog, she opened the cooler and handed CW a Hershey bar.

He should say no. A voice in his head warned that accepting this gift could be the beginning of a much bigger adventure.

But CW liked adventures.

He peeled back the wrapper and took a bite. Loon Lake wasn't an uptight kind of town. Suppose it didn't hurt to make nice with the newcomers before he enforced the Animal Control ordinances. What could happen by eating a chocolate bar?

Lena smiled at him.

For the love of Pete, she was a pretty woman. She reminded him of that *Law & Order* actress, but shorter and rounder.

But dating women with kids, not the kind of adventure he'd been willing to try so far. The boy was kinda cute, though.

Chip the dog, surely named just this morning if the wood chips in his coat were any indication, whined a few feet away.

CW reached for an appropriate tone of authority. He was in charge here. "Your dog looks hungry. Why don't you get him some dog food and then tie him up?" He looked closer, trying to see under the mud and debris. "And he needs a collar and license."

"Oh, well, I — I just ran out of dog food this morning, actually. I — *we*," she looked toward her son, "were just going grocery shopping when you came by."

Ri-ight. He knew her "tell" now, stuttering and looking away. He decided to humor her.

"Well, he doesn't look choosy. Why don't you put something in his food dish and bring it out here. Animals almost always come when there's food in their dish."

He bet Lena had a dog bowl for that muddy mess of a beast like he had pink, frilly sheets on his bed.

"Right. Of course." She squirmed under his gaze. "His dish is, um—" She looked around the back yard, her gaze slipping over the back wall of the garage and over to the sliding glass door.

CW crossed his arms again and tried to pretend he wasn't having fun. "So let me get this straight. *Your dog* won't come when he's called, looks like he's been running in the woods for a month, and could probably inhale the lion's share of a 24-ounce steak. But you just happen to be out of dog food, his bowl is at the cleaners, and he lost his collar and license while he was on vacation without you."

That got her dander up.

"Listen, buddy." Lena pulled herself up to her full height and faced him, her nose near his chin. "I may have just moved here, and obviously I have some things to learn about how things work in Loon Lake."

CW wondered if steam would pour out of her ears.

"But if my son and I say that's our dog, then that's our dog." She looked toward the window again and smiled and waved. Under the smile, she spoke with gritted teeth. "And if you make Joey cry, I swear I'll make you explain to him why you're such a meany."

A meany? CW hadn't been called a meany since the second grade.

He was going to have to get caps on his teeth. He was grinding the enamel right off them in his effort not to double over in laughter. He had to get out of here before he lost it.

"Well, ma'am, dogs without a license get picked up and taken to the shelter. That's my job. You have forty-eight hours to get your dog licensed. The office is in the government building off Sunset." He couldn't help himself from adding the next bit. "Next door to the Sheriff's Department."

CW saluted the woman with his chocolate bar, turned on his heel and walked back to his truck. The warmth he felt on his back could've been from the rising sun. But he was pretty sure it was emanating from the ready-to-blow volcano behind him.

WHEN LENA HEARD THE TRUCK PULL AWAY, SHE SIGHED AND put her hands on her hips. She'd just lied, several times, to an authority figure *in front of her son*. What kind of mother did that? She mock glared at the dog. "Lotta help you are. If you want to be fed around here, you're going to have to pretend you're part of the family."

Joey gave a whoop behind her from the open back door. "I knew it! Thanks, Mom!" He raced around the tent in circles.

Lena watched the dog carefully, looking for any sign of aggression. But Chip was panting happily for the first time, dancing in circles at a distance, his tongue lolling out of his mouth. A mouth that surely would like more food. Lena considered the contents of her refrigerator, but decided the dogcatcher was right. Dog food was the order of the day.

"Get some clothes on, buddy, let's go get him some dog

food." She picked up a few things from the camping area to take into the house, especially anything the dog could get into and eat. Turning to look at him, she said, "Chip, stay." She was probably wasting her breath. But the dog sat. Close enough.

They drove to the nearby convenience store, The Laughing Loon. An older man greeted them and said dog food was in aisle three. Lena looked over the choices and bought two cans of a mid-priced soft food, and a small bag of mid-priced dry food. No point in being stingy and buying something the animal wouldn't eat. But why waste money if he were here today and gone tomorrow?

Joey tried to add a collar and leash and dog bowl, but Lena suggested they wait and see whether Chip wanted to stay. "He wants to," Joey assured her. "God sent him, 'member?"

She smiled. Child-like faith. How could she put a damper on that? Besides, Loon Lake was their chance at happiness. Joey looked ecstatic at the prospect of becoming a dog owner. Lena didn't have it in her to explain to him how the world worked, like that dogs needed to be fed and walked and picked up after — and sometimes they ran away or died. "Okay, go ahead."

Joey grabbed the blue collar, green leash and yellow dog food bowl he'd been looking at.

"Don't you want to get a matching collar and leash?"

Joey scrunched up his face. "Why?" He strode to the counter with his purchases.

Men. Apparently it was a Y chromosome thing.

"Whatcha got there, young man?" The gentleman behind the counter grabbed the dog bowl before it crashed to the floor.

"We got a dog!" Joey's face lit up. Lena feared she'd let him have ten dogs just to see that look on his face every day. She didn't know if Joey knew what he was missing by not having a dad, but even at five he knew he was missing something.

"You did?" The man's eyes crinkled at the edges as he smiled at Lena. "What kind of dog is it?"

"Well, um," Joey twisted back and forth, hanging onto the counter, squishing his face up as he considered the question. "I guess we'll give him a bath and find out."

Oh dear. Lena felt her face grow warm. She just moved here and now people knew she was picking up strays. There was something embarrassing about that.

"The dog man came to help us, but he couldn't catch Chip," Joey continued. "Maybe he's not very good with dogs."

"Okay, Joey, why don't you go get us a carton of orange juice for breakfast, right over there. Thanks, buddy."

Lena tried to pretend she wasn't embarrassed as she pulled out her wallet. She hadn't been raised in a picking-up-strays kind of household. If her parents had ever wanted a dog, she was sure they would've bought one from a breeder. She smiled at the man behind the counter and fumbled for something to say. "I'm Lena Hart. We're new."

"Willie Larson. Pleased to make your acquaintance." The man opened a brown paper bag with a snap and began loading it. "So you met C-Dubb this morning."

"I'm sorry?"

"C-Dubb, that's what the boys around here call him. CW. Charlie Emerson. Good kid. Well," Willie laughed. "Maybe not so much a kid anymore."

"Ah, yes, we met."

Willie raised his eyebrows and chuckled.

Something in her tone must've given her away. Like the fact that she didn't care for Mr. Emerson's domineering attitude, the way he walked in and took charge of everything. Nor the way he stared at her behind when he thought she couldn't see. She particularly didn't like that she was curious how he looked when he smiled.

Willie leaned toward her with a conspiratorial whisper. "He's a lot of bluster. A real jelly donut. High school football heroes are still revered in small towns, that's all."

Before Lena could figure out what a suitable reply should be, Joey was back with the orange juice. His tongue stuck out as he hefted it up onto the counter.

Willie reached into a jar of red licorice sticks and pulled one out. "Now don't let your momma know," he said in a stage whisper as he handed it to Joey, "but this is a little 'Welcome to Loon Lake' present for you."

Lena nodded when Joey looked to her for permission. She smiled at Willie. What an adorable man. If CW were so kind, she'd have a totally different opinion of him.

Driving home, she let her mind wander. She'd go get a license for Chip as soon as she thought he'd stick around. Would CW come back and check? Or would he look her up in his computer to see if she'd come in yet? She hoped this dog wouldn't be the beginning of trouble for her. She and Joey wanted to live friendly, quiet lives in a friendly, quiet town. Constant meetings with the local dogcatcher wouldn't be her idea of a friendly, quiet life.

Unless they just happened to meet around town. A jelly donut, huh? He did have that football player look, now that she thought about it. Big barrel chest, strong arms, his hair cut short and slightly spiky. He might be a little cute out of that grey city uniform.

"Mom?"

"Mmm?" She needed to insert some kind of father figure in Joey's life. Her parents lived in Florida, a place she enjoyed visiting but not a place she'd want to live. Tim's dad died when he was a teenager. Maybe there was a Big Brothers program up here. Otherwise, for Joey to have a dad in his life, she would have to have a husband in hers.

But she didn't want a new one. She liked the last one. A lot. And she missed him. How did one go about choosing another?

"I talked to God this morning and told him thanks for giving me Chip."

"That's good, honey. Thanking God is very important."

Maybe there was some way to meet people and make friends in a less awkward way than "dating." Maybe she'd meet people at the PTA. Of course, most of them would be married. Perhaps Joey would make friends with a boy whose father invited Joey to go fishing with them, too. If she volunteered at church, she'd meet people. Or maybe she should put the idea right out of her mind. Joey had a dog now. He didn't need a dad, yet.

"How long do I have to wait before I ask him for something else?"

"Ask who, baby?" Lena pulled into the driveway, still surprised that she now lived someplace where a gravel driveway was a step up from one's neighbors. She wondered what her dad would say when he and Mom came to visit.

"God." Joey grabbed the bag with the dog collar and leash.

"You don't have to wait. You can ask him anything, anytime you want." Lena unlocked the door, wondering if Chip was still in the backyard. "He may not answer the way you want, but you can talk to God about anything."

"Okay, be right back."

Lena watched in surprise as her son marched to his room and shut the door. *Okay.* Something he wanted more than the dog in his back yard? She shook her head, put the juice away, and opened a can of dog food.

She scanned the yard as she opened the sliding glass door. Nothing. *Oh please, God, don't let the dog have disappeared.* Joey was so easy to please. She really wanted him to have a dog if that would make him happy. The thought popped up that maybe she was so willing because she secretly wanted a dog, too. What if God really did send Chip to them? That would mean he didn't belong to anyone else. And that he'd stick around.

She tried to whistle, but only an airy, watery kind of noise came out. No dog came running to that ridiculous sound. How could she never have learned to whistle, Tim used to tease her.

Guess now was the time to see if Chip knew God had sent him to Joey. "Chip! Here boy," she called. "Breakfast is ready, Chip."

Come on, Chip. You can do it. She scanned the back yard and the side woods where she'd first seen him. *Come on, Chip.*

Lena heard the sliding door open and Joey came out. *Come on, Chip. Don't disappoint my son. You'll never get another hot dog out of me again.*

"Where is he, Mom?" Joey looked around.

She thought fast. "Maybe he's waiting for you to call him."

Joey look a long deep breath and yelled, "Chiiip!"

Lena put one hand over her ear. *Ow.*

They waited. A moment later, a crashing sound came from the woods on the right. They both turned.

"Come on, Chip! Come get breakfast," Joey yelled again. He laughed as Chip burst through the underbrush, and looked at Lena as if to say, isn't having a dog come when you call the best thing ever?

Lena laughed in relief and set the dog bowl down about ten feet away. Chip's expression looked like he was as happy to be there as Joey was to have him. He skidded to a stop at the bowl and inhaled the can of food. Then he trotted over to Joey, sat down in front of him, cocked his head and put out his paw.

Lena and Joey stared at him in wonder. "Well, someone

loved you once," she said quietly as she shook Chip's paw. "What happened?"

She showed Joey how to shake and in minutes, the two were happily absorbed in each other. Lena watched for a few minutes. Then, deciding it was safe to leave them alone for a moment, she picked up the dog bowl and opened the door.

"Mom?"

She turned back with a smile. "Yes?"

"I talked to God again and told Him we wanted a new dad, too."

We?

He giggled as Chip licked his ear. "And God said yes."

IT TOOK THE REST OF THE DAY TO SET UP A SPOT TO WASH Chip, get the dog to allow them to wash him, and get him fairly dry before dirt stuck to his wet fur and they had to start all over again.

When two pairs of begging eyes locked Lena in their gaze, she gave in with a laugh and a sigh. "Fine, he can come in the house." Joey cheered and Chip let out his first bark. "*But*," and she pointed her finger at her son just like her mother used to point her finger at Lena, "you have to take him out every hour — *every hour, Joey* — until we know for sure he's housebroken."

Boy and dog were halfway in the back door already. Joey called out, "I will, Mom," and then they were gone.

"And not on the furniture!" Lena yelled. "Oh, dear me," she muttered to herself as she picked up the towels and her half-empty bottle of Herbal Essence shampoo. Chip now smelled like orchids but at least his fur was moisturized. She should Google "dog care." Should she buy a flea collar? Dog shampoo? "What have I gotten myself into?"

The mindless movements of cleanup allowed her mind to wander. *A dad?* God said yes to a dad? Lena shook her head. Of course God hadn't said yes. Joey heard what he wanted to hear.

But God seemed to have sent him a dog, so...

Without warning, an image of the dogcatcher came to mind. CW Emerson. Emerson, like one of Lena's favorite poets. But a football player. Not really the type she'd been interested in in the past. Tim ran track in high school and was on the chess team in college. They talked about world events and went to art galleries.

What would she talk about with a dogcatcher?

You're allowing your prejudices to take over because you think he's cute.

Cute? No. Maybe. He did have a certain quality to him. Lena felt a little smile starting. She clamped her lips down on it. She was getting carried away by the hopes of a little boy. *Enough already.* Besides, she reminded herself, he's a bit too overbearing for my taste.

THE NEXT MORNING, LENA LOADED JOEY AND CHIP INTO THE car — the dog's manners had proven to be quite acceptable so far — and drove to the vet. She'd made a few calls and found out he needed a rabies shot before he could get a license. That done, she ignored the reproachful looks of her two charges ("I hate shots," Joey grumbled when Chip got his) and drove to the Sheriff's Department. She found a parking spot, noticed happily that she didn't have to pay a meter in her new hometown, and marched her two wards into the county office.

She followed the signs for dog licenses down a short hall and up to an unmanned counter. "You want to ring the bell?" She lifted Joey up and he hit the bell four or five times before she could get him back to the floor. "Enough! We don't want to be rude."

"Coming," a man called.

A moment later, who should appear but CW Emerson and the head of a deer.

Lena shrank back. An actual deer. A formerly live animal now attached, in part, to a piece of varnished wood. Lena felt her face twist into an expression of horror and disgust. She'd never seen one this close before. Country living. She had to get over it or alienate all her neighbors. She ripped her eyes away from the carcass and crashed into CW's gaze.

He looked alarmed and backed up a step. "You gonna be sick?"

Lena willed herself to regain a neutral expression. It was infinitely easier when CW put the deer's head on a desk behind him. If she kept her focus on the live man, she couldn't see the dead head.

"Fine, fine," she muttered. She floundered for a topic — any topic — that would get her mind off the deer. "What are you doing here? You catch dogs and sell the licenses too?" She sounded to her own ears like she was on the offensive, but she was still trying to get that deer out of her mind.

"It's a Loon Lake scam, you caught us."

For a moment, Lena wasn't sure what to say. Then she noticed the crinkles around his eyes. A smile burst out when she realized he was teasing her. "Ha, ha. I'm here to..." She started to say, I'm here to get the dog's license, but she stopped when she realized yesterday she'd implied that the dog had a license and had lost it. She'd expected some new stranger to be behind the counter. Someone she wouldn't have to lie to in order to save face.

"Let me guess." CW leaned over the counter, resting his elbows disconcertingly close to Lena. "Hey there, sport. I see you found your dog under all that mud, huh?"

He had a pleasant voice. Nicer than yesterday. Friendlier, especially when he spoke to Joey and the dog. Lena smiled.

CW turned toward her just then and caught her smile.

She tried to stop, lowering her head so he couldn't see her expression, trying to think of something normal, something professional to say in conversation. Before she could stutter anything, anything *at all* would've been fine, he grinned at her. She saw it out of the corner of her eye and her gaze met his like a magnet. It hit her in the chest and reignited her smile without her permission. Apparently the part of her that reacted to his flirting wasn't looking for her mind's permission. Was it her imagination, or did his eyes dart to her empty ring finger?

"So, you know what kind of dog you have now?" he asked her.

Lena rolled her eyes at him. "I've always known what kind of dog I have." She looked at Chip. Black and white, now that he was clean, with beautiful long hair that was going to make a mess of her carpets. "He's a collie."

CW raised his eyebrows.

"Kind of a collie-mutt mix." She gauged CW's reaction out of the corner of her eye. He didn't look like he agreed with her assessment. "Mongrel sort of thing, with a, uh..." Collies were brown and white, come to think of it. "A black and white dog in the mix."

"Are you trying to say 'border collie' by chance?" He looked younger when he was laughing.

Lena wondered how old he was. She could feel the warmth from his shoulder so close to her own, but she refused to move away. It would be an admission that he bothered her, and he didn't. "I guess you might call him a border collie," she hedged.

CW laughed. "I would because he is. Mostly, I'd say."

He stood upright again and tapped a key on his computer. "So you want to register him?" He looked at her. "Or just get a new tag? You said you lost his?"

Caught. He'd look in the computer and know she'd never registered this dog or any other in Loon Lake. Or anywhere else. No way to win this, darn it. She hated losing. "I said *he* lost his license. I wasn't wearing it. I didn't lose it."

CW grinned. "Ah. So he isn't your dog?"

"He most certainly is." Lena tried to put some backbone behind her words. For reasons she didn't understand, this man brought out her competitive streak and she didn't want him to win this argument. But he also made her smile. If she could feel a smile pulling at her mouth, he could certainly see it.

"You mean, *now* he's your dog."

"No, from the first moment I said it, he's been my dog." Lena suspected she was flirting since the argument was getting kind of fun. Yikes. *Theoretically*, she wanted to find Joey a new dad, but practically speaking, it was a whole different ball game. A game she wasn't sure she was ready to play yet.

"He's *my* dog, mister," Joey piped up from the floor where he was shaking Chip's paw over and over again.

The confounded dogcatcher looked at Lena and cocked his head toward Joey. "You're not going to blame this on him, are you?" he whispered.

Lena pressed her lips together to keep from laughing. "This is our dog. Yesterday, *the dogcatcher* told us we needed a dog license. Can you help us or not? Do you even work here?" No uniform, no badge, no name tag. Maybe he was just walking by the desk. She checked out his biceps stretching his navy blue T-shirt. Much better than the grey uniform.

"Some days," he said as he keyed something into the computer. "Am I looking for an old license, or do you want to start over and get a new one? Now that he's your dog, I mean." His eyes crinkled again.

Lena finally gave in and laughed. "Fine, you win. One

new license, please." She put an excessive amount of sugar in the last few words.

CW shot her a knowing look. He grinned at her and typed. "And I believe you named him Chip yesterday. Do you want to think about it some more, or is that the name you want?"

Lena felt her face growing red. When was the last time a man had teased her this way? Years. She couldn't remember. Tim didn't tease much, he was just sweet and easygoing. CW, on the other hand, didn't seem to stop.

She rather liked it.

Lena nudged her son with her foot. "Is Chip a good name for your dog, Joey?"

He looked up with a frown. "That's his *name*, Mom."

She looked to CW. "That's his *name*," she repeated quietly.

He chuckled with her and typed some more. Then he tipped his head to her. "And your name is Lena, right?"

Butterflies tickled the inside of her stomach. "Yeah." She cleared her throat, rattled. "Yes. Lena Hart. L-E-N-A H-A-R-T."

"At 2855 Maple Street."

"Mmm-hmm."

"And your phone number?" CW fixed her with a look that seemed to be asking more than what the government required.

Could he be interested in her? Like, to call her in a non-dog-related matter? The butterflies circled. She gave him her number.

He smiled while he typed. What did that mean? Would he call her? Did she want him to? Lena had no idea what to think. Time to leave.

She pulled out her debit card. "So how much do I owe you?" She paid for the license, and CW assured her it would be in the mail next week.

"Be sure to keep him in your yard. If he goes outside the

Loon Lake area and someone else picks him up, they won't know who to call without the license."

Lena nodded and gathered up her things. "All right, guys, time to go."

Joey scrambled up. "Bye, Dogcatcher-Man!" He waved.

Chip wagged his tail. The dog didn't look too put out to have a collar and leash on, not even a mismatched set. But Lena was sure the dog hadn't met her eye since the rabies shot.

CW leaned over the counter and high-fived Joey. "Bye, little man. Take good care of your dog now." He smiled at Lena again. "And your mom."

"I will," Joey shouted as he ran down the hall with Chip.

"See ya around," he said to Lena.

"Yeah." She smiled at his chin, suddenly shy. "Yes, I'm sure. See you around." Stumbling over her words, she gave up and followed her son, hoping she wouldn't stumble over her feet as well.

All her theoretical plans for what kind of life she and Joey would have when they moved to Loon Lake were coming together quicker and less theoretically than Lena had anticipated. She was still trying to catch her breath as she walked out the door.

AT HOME, LENA MADE SANDWICHES AND OPENED HER LAPTOP. They looked up "owning your first dog" on Google. When she read that people food isn't good for dogs, she and Joey both finished the rest of their sandwiches on their own. Chip sighed in disapproval. Before she could give Joey any more valuable advice about what to do or not do with a new dog, he and Chip raced out the sliding glass door to the back yard.

Having a dog and a five-year-old at the same time was

more exhausting than Lena had expected. If she wasn't cleaning up after one, she was reprimanding the other. By the time she put in a movie after dinner, she was ready for a break.

"Which will it be, buddy? *The Iron Giant* or *Monster House?*"

"*Iron Giant!*" her son yelled. "Chip, you're really going to like this one. Don't be scared though, 'cause the giant isn't really bad."

Chip licked Joey's hand and Joey giggled.

"No licking, Chip." Lena had no idea if the dog understood what she said, but he lowered his head a little and raised his eyebrows as if in apology. Lena looked away before she smiled. "Good dog," she added.

Since Chip wasn't allowed on the couch, Joey decided to sit with him on the floor. He wrapped his arm around the dog's neck as he explained the movie to his canine friend. When the giant was safely ensconced in the junkyard, eating his fill of broken down cars, Lena finally let her eyes drift closed.

Joey was so happy, and that made her happy, but for heaven's sake, it was like having two kids. Alone. She sighed. Earlier Joey had added to his monologue about dads.

"It'll be easier to find a dad now," he'd told her. "Justin has a dog and he has a dad."

Lena had tried to explain to him that his friend already had a dad when he got the dog. But a five-year-old's sense of logic was difficult to argue with.

Her mind wandered as she felt herself drifting to sleep. She'd at least try, for Joey's sake. Maybe she'd meet someone. CW Emerson's face appeared in her mind. Maybe she'd go out with him if he called. Months from now, no need to hurry. Maybe they'd have fun...

Lena fell asleep and dreamed of dogcatchers and dogs and wondered why the dogs were all whining. What was CW doing to make them so unhappy? The whining got louder and a dog barked. Lena woke with a start.

She rubbed her eyes and looked around. The movie was still playing, almost to the part when the giant flies up to intercept the missile and save the town. But the whining from her dream continued. It was Chip. She looked down to see the dog half covered by her sleeping son. Maybe he didn't like having Joey's weight on him.

She leaned over the couch to shake Joey awake and take him to bed. That's when it finally pierced her consciousness that some of the wheezing sounds in her dream were coming from her son.

"Joey?" She fell to her knees and lifted him off Chip. The dog immediately rose and licked Lena's hand, whining again.

Her son's breath was coming in shallow gasps, wheezing in and out. She'd never heard anything like it. "Joey, come on, wake up." She held him upright against her shoulder, thinking that would help him breathe easier. But the sound in her ear only frightened her more. What was happening? Had he choked on something?

Involuntarily, the memory of rushing to the hospital to find Tim near death overwhelmed her. She couldn't lose Joey, too. She shook him, trying to think of what she should do. Her mind went blank. She needed help. Where was the hospital?

She hurried to the phone, murmuring comforting words to Joey as her voice rose in panic. She dialed 911.

"Nine-one-one, what is your emergency?"

"My son, he's not breathing right, I need to know where the hospital is!"

"What's your address, ma'am?"

Lena tried to calm down, but she couldn't remember their new address. Another picture of Tim lying lifeless in a hospital bed raced through her mind, pausing just long enough to add to her fear. "Just tell me where the hospital is!"

"I can send an ambulance to your address. Are you calling from 2855 Maple Street?"

"Yes! How do I get to the hospital from here?" Why hadn't she found out where the hospital was when she moved in? What kind of mother doesn't know where the hospital is? What should she do? She needed to do something to help Joey. Lena felt herself sobbing. She couldn't understand the operator.

Another memory surfaced, a friend telling her about sitting in the bathroom for hours with the hot water running to help her colicky baby breathe.

She ran to the bathroom and turned on the shower. She heard the operator say an ambulance was on the way. When the water got hot, she opened the shower curtain and closed the door so the steam would build up. She'd forgotten that the shower head needed to be replaced. Water and steam sprayed across the bathroom, soaking Lena and Joey. She didn't care, not if it would help her son breathe.

She heard Chip whine outside the closed bathroom door. Was Joey's breathing getting easier? Or worse? What seemed like ages later, the dog barked from another part of the house. Lena opened the door at the sound of voices and Chip's scratching. Two EMTs rushed toward her. She sobbed with relief.

"Please, there's something wrong with his breathing." She struggled to speak rationally. They would help her. Joey would be okay. He would.

"Lena, it's going to be all right," a man said. "I'm CW, remember? I'm trained in first aid, I'm here to help." He reached for Joey.

She tried to focus on the man and recognized the animal control officer, her dogcatcher. Had she dialed the wrong number? Conjured him from her dreams? She held Joey tighter, turning away from CW's open arms. "No, no, he needs a hospital, doctors, he needs—"

"Ma'am," the other man interrupted, "we can help. But you need to give us your boy."

Lena looked in confusion at CW.

"Lena," he said calmly, "we're with the volunteer fire department. We're both certified EMTs. It's okay. Can you give me Joey so we can help him?"

She understood now. She did. She just couldn't get her arms to turn over her son. CW stepped forward and gently pulled him from her arms. Another sob escaped. *He'll be okay. He'll be fine.* She had to get hold of herself.

She felt Chip lick her hand and she patted his head. "Good dog," she whispered. She grabbed a couple towels and followed CW and his partner out to the living room. They lay Joey down on the floor and started to examine him.

"Is he allergic to anything?" CW asked.

"N-no, I don't think so." Lena held the towels tightly against her chest, afraid to get in the way.

"Does he have any respiratory problems like asthma?" the other man asked.

"Asthma? I don't — I don't know. I mean, no, nothing that I..." She'd heard of asthma going undetected until a sudden attack. Is that what happened? Or did he choke on something? He wasn't eating when the movie started. She shouldn't have fallen asleep. If it wasn't for Chip, who knows how long—

Chip. She found him at her elbow and put her arms around the dog. "Good boy. Good boy, Chip. Good job."

CW spoke to her. "Lena, we're going to take him to the hospital. A doctor will meet us at the door. Why don't you get your purse and anything you need. You can ride with me, okay? With us," he corrected.

She nodded. Everything was going to be fine. Just fine. A doctor would meet them. A doctor would know what to do. She looked at Joey, lying on the floor, looking small and vulnerable with an oxygen mask on. Was it her imagination or was he breathing easier?

"Is he going to be okay?" She looked to CW, now the person she trusted most.

"He's going to be fine. The doctor will help him get his breathing back to normal. Are you ready?"

The men moved Joey to a gurney, and she grabbed her purse.

While his partner drove the ambulance, CW stayed in the back with Joey and Lena. When he took her hand, she gripped it hard.

"Everything's going to be fine," he said. He sounded so sure.

"I know." Lena bit back a sob. "It's just that it-it reminds me of another time."

She didn't like to think about it. A car accident on the way home from work. Lena was at a play date for Joey and didn't get the call from the hospital for nearly an hour. By the time she arrived, she and Tim had enough time to say goodbye and then he was gone.

It seemed too personal, too private to tell a virtual stranger about Tim's death. But she couldn't get it out of her mind. It had been months since she'd had one of her grief episodes, as she'd been calling them.

The pressure burst out in another sob and the tears poured down. She waited for CW to try to comfort her, shush her, like her friends and family did. She knew she'd be embarrassed as soon as he did or said anything. But he only increased the pressure on her hand and let her cry. It made her want to hug him.

The episode passed as quickly as it began. CW handed her a tissue and she wiped her face. "Thanks," she said.

"It happens." He looked out the window. "We're here." He moved back into brisk EMT mode as he helped wheel Joey into the Loon Lake Hospital.

Lena felt somewhat comforted that she'd already met CW before tonight. Somehow it made the situation easier, easier to trust all these strangers with her only child.

It didn't take long for Dr. Robert Dillon to examine her son, order some tests, and reassure her that Joey was breathing comfortably again. A quiet ER must be another gift of small town living, tonight anyway. Probably an allergic reaction, the doctor said. They should make an appointment for some allergy tests, and meanwhile keep an eye on him. Lena sagged against the hospital bed in relief, her hand never leaving her little boy. Her baby.

Dr. Dillon touched Lena's shoulder. "Why don't you take him home now, get some rest."

It was all Lena could do not to throw her arms around the tall, white-haired man and sob her gratitude.

CW approached her a half hour later as she gathered an exhausted Joey into her arms, the last of the paperwork signed, the ordeal nearly behind her. "How you doing?"

"Better, thanks." She held Joey close, feeling him breathe against her. She could finally breathe again, too.

"Doc says you can take him home. I figured you could use a ride."

Lena offered a small smile. "I think one ambulance ride tonight is enough."

"Volunteers, remember? The ambulance stays here at the hospital. My truck's outside. I don't mind, really."

Lena considered her options. There probably weren't any taxis in Loon Lake. And at least she sort of knew him. "Thanks, CW. I appreciate it."

IT DIDN'T TAKE LONG TO GET BACK HOME. LENA LIKED HOW

close everything was here. No rush hour traffic. Everything within a few miles. Country life might grow on her.

She looked at the man in the driver seat. "How exactly is it that you're the dogcatcher, the dog license, uh, man, and an EMT?"

"Small town, lots of part-time jobs." CW smiled at her and checked on Joey in the rearview mirror. "Life never gets boring. Though I have to say, I don't usually run into the same person over and over again."

He reached across the seat and took her hand. Surprised, Lena wasn't sure how she should react. After the events of the last few hours, though, she could use the comfort of another's touch. She turned to the back seat. Joey rested in a child seat CW had borrowed from the hospital.

"That's why I moved here, you know. To add some excitement to your small town."

CW glanced over at her and chuckled. "Well, us Loon Lake folks have a high tolerance for adventure. Just so you know."

At her house, CW suggested Lena go unlock the door and he'd carry Joey in. She started to argue that he was heavy, then stopped herself. If a nice man wanted to help carry her burdens for one night, she should just say thank you.

She opened the door and directed CW to Joey's room. Then she changed her mind. "No, put him in my bed. I want to watch him tonight." CW wisely didn't argue with her.

She turned on the light in her room — and gritted her teeth at the boxes still piled everywhere. She hadn't planned for company. "Sorry about the mess. Haven't unpacked everything yet." She swiped at a lacy pink bra and tossed it under a pillow. She hoped CW hadn't seen it.

She pulled down the bedspread and sheets, and CW eased past her to lay Joey down. Her son muttered something in his sleep and Lena saw CW smile. He brushed his hand over her son's forehead and whispered something back.

"What'd he say?"

CW stood up, unnervingly close in the space between boxes and bed. He smiled at his shoes and wiped a hand over his chin. "Just talking in his sleep is all."

Lena stepped past CW to kiss her son and pull the sheet up. "Are you sure he's okay?"

"He'll be fine, Lena. I promise."

She sighed and chose to believe him. The alternatives wouldn't allow her to sleep. She brushed her hand over Joey's hair and followed CW out to the kitchen.

She looked at the time on the microwave. "I'd offer you a drink to say thank you, but I think coffee at midnight is probably a bad idea."

"Agreed." CW shuffled his feet. "I could stop by tomorrow and see how you're doing. How Joey's doing."

"That'd be nice." How could she say that she'd like him to come over without actually saying the words? "I'd appreciate that." Lena wondered if this was the way all single moms met someone new. As Joey would say, it was really weird.

She heard whining and scratching at the sliding glass door. "Oh, Chip, I should let him in. And buy some doggie treats tomorrow." She opened the door and unclipped his leash. "Maybe I'll buy you doggie treats for the rest of your life," she said as she scrubbed at his ears and head and neck. "What a good dog you are. God did send you, didn't he? Didn't he? You're such a good dog."

Chip groaned in pleasure and pressed against her legs.

"What's that?" CW asked from behind her.

Lena moved a bit and CW bent down and scratched Chip's ears, too. "Joey said he prayed for a dog and God sent him Chip. I thought it was sweet and cute, but now I'm beginning to think 'out of the mouths of babes' and all that."

"God sent him?" CW looked surprised. Maybe even alarmed.

"He thinks Chip is an answer to prayer."

"Huh." CW was quiet while he rubbed Chip's back and sides.

Chip looked exceptionally pleased with all the attention.

As the silence continued, Lena wondered if prayer was a taboo subject for CW. That would be unfortunate since it was a pretty basic part of their lives.

"Listen, I better go and let you get some sleep." CW stood and headed for the door. Did he seem distracted, or just tired?

Lena let him out, watching as he walked toward his truck. "Thanks again," she called out quietly, trying not to wake the neighbors.

He raised his hand. "I'll see you tomorrow."

Impulsively, Lena said, "Stop by for lunch."

CW grinned and opened his truck door. "I'll see you then."

DID GOD SEND YOU TO BE MY DAD?

CW couldn't get the words out of his head. They'd sounded cute coming from the sleepy boy's mouth, but when his thoughts turned to the kid's mom... Lena Hart was pretty and sassy and funny. Maybe he shouldn't, in this day and age, but he liked being there for her, saving the day and having her lean on him. It made him feel... Well, he liked it is all.

That didn't necessarily mean God put them all together. Of course, based on some of the strange ways God answered prayers in CW's experience, he wouldn't put it past him.

He pulled into Lena's driveway a few minutes before noon the next day hoping he wasn't too early. City lunch time or country lunch time? Was he acting too interested by being early? He was in between calls, though, so it made sense to stop by now. He pulled his keys from the ignition and tapped his fingers on the steering wheel. Go in or go home.

He sat a couple moments longer.

Come on, man, go in or go home.

He went in.

"Hi!" Joey came running when CW rang the doorbell. "You're here for lunch! We've been cooking all day!" He flung open the screen door.

"Hey there, sport, how you feeling?" CW ruffled Joey's hair. That's when the smell of chocolate overtook his senses. *Wow.*

He turned to Lena when she walked around the corner. She looked real nice, a picture of summer in light blue shorts and a sleeveless yellow blouse tied at her waist. He was glad he'd decided to change out of his uniform in favor of a nice button-down short sleeve shirt. He took a step closer to her and smiled. "Your house smells like chocolate."

It looked as if she were blushing. That or it was really hot in the kitchen. He decided to believe what he wanted.

"I felt like making brownies," she said, twisting her hands at her waist. Then, as if she'd decided that sounded wrong, she added, "I mean, I wanted to thank you and brownies seemed a good way to go."

"I love brownies," he said. She stood close enough that he could smell flowers. He didn't move. She smiled at him. CW didn't go dancing much, an occasional go at line-dancing, but it occurred to him that Lena would be the perfect height to dance with. The top of her head came to about eye level on him.

Joey pushed his way between them and spoke with the energy that can only be attributed to a child who heals quickly. "I helped! I made brownies, too! And-and-and we made strawberry salad! But it's not really salad, it's really cottage cheese, and it's my favorite! And now we're going to make...to make," he paused and turned to his mother. "What are we making now, Mom?"

Lena put her hand on Joey's head and said to CW, "I

thought we'd have sandwiches out on the back patio, if that's all right with you."

"Yeah, and we can each make our own!" Joey crowed in excitement.

"That's about the most perfect summer lunch I can think of," he said to Joey.

"Yeah!" The kid was excited to be the center of attention.

"Okay, go wash your hands now," Lena said as she turned him toward the hallway. "And don't touch Chip after you wash," she called. She turned back to CW and chuckled nervously. "Sorry, we don't have a lot of company."

"I'm sure you'll be making friends right and left soon." He cleared his throat and looked at his hands, then stuffed them in his pockets. He pulled them out. What was he doing here? He was no Jax Edgerly, Loon Lake's own ladies man. CW wasn't sure what to do in a non-crisis with a pretty woman.

Lena gestured toward the kitchen. "Do you want to...?"

"Yeah, sure," he agreed quickly.

He followed her. When was an appropriate time to ask her out? Maybe he should wait till another day. But she seemed like she might say yes now. He tried to focus on lunch.

Joey came back and chattered on about the food, the things Chip was learning (which CW suspected Chip had learned someplace else), and how great it was going to be to go to kindergarten.

"We get to play *all day!*"

Lena shooed him out the sliding door with his plate. She took a deep breath and then looked at CW and laughed. "Because, you know, he doesn't get to play *all day* at home."

CW laughed with her. "You're a good mom."

She looked down at the counter and handed him a plate. "Well, I..."

"You are. Trust me. I've got one. I know what I'm talking about."

Lena looked over her shoulder at him and laughed. "Well, thank you. I appreciate that, especially after last night."

"Things happen," CW assured her. "Especially with kids. I know. I'm there a lot of the time. You couldn't have foreseen something like this."

"I suppose." She didn't sound convinced.

CW put his hand on her shoulder. "You'll be fine. *He'll* be fine."

Lena turned to him. "I just wanted you to know how much I appreciate you. Last night was..." She looked away, then seemed to muster her courage and met his gaze again.

He moved half a step closer. She smelled better than the brownies. "You don't have to thank me. I was happy to help."

She smiled and looked a little uncomfortable.

"But if you want to keep making brownies to thank me," he said to make her laugh, "I won't say no."

It worked. She laughed. "Well, you should taste them first."

CW knew right then what he wanted to taste. If she wasn't some kid's mom, a kid who was only feet away and separated from them by a glass door, he knew exactly what he'd do. He'd lean down like this...

She didn't move away. In fact, she seemed to stop breathing for a moment. Her eyes lowered and he knew she was staring at his lips. Same way he was staring at hers.

Another inch. She didn't say no. Didn't back up. No child yelling in the background to leave his mother alone, as he'd once done.

CW leaned his head closer. She was the perfect height for kissing. His lips touched hers and he felt her breathe again. She was warm and smelled of birthdays and celebrations.

Lena rested her hand on his forearm. He moved one hand to her waist and she moved closer. The kiss was unlike any other CW had shared. This one wasn't about going faster, but enjoying the moment. It was satisfying in a way he couldn't express.

They pulled back at the same time, laughed in a slightly embarrassed way at the same time, smiled at each other at the same time.

"I was thinking," CW had to say it before he lost his nerve, before she started second-guessing the kiss, "maybe I could take you two out to Jimmy's Pizza one night. Or maybe," he tried not to sound as unsure as he felt, "I could take you to a little Italian place here in town sometime."

Lena blushed. He could tell for sure this time. "I'd like that," she said.

CW felt an old familiar urge to throw a ball down on the turf, thrust his arms into the air, and whoop it up. He felt like he'd won something important, or been given something precious.

It occurred to him that he did a lot of rescuing in his jobs, people and animals both. But kissing Lena Hart made him feel like she had rescued him.

A PEEK AT LOVE AT THE FLUFF AND FOLD

A STRAYS OF LOON LAKE ROMANTIC COMEDY, AVAILABLE NOW AT MAJOR ONLINE RETAILERS

*W*ilfred Larson buttoned his shirt and glanced up at his doctor. "So? What's the verdict, Dill?"

Dr. Bob Dillon, Dill to his friends, wrote a few notes on Willie's chart and said, "Clean bill of health. As always. Should have plenty of fishing in your future."

"Wanna take the boat out tonight?" If there was one activity Willie loved most, it was fishing. Trout, bass, walleye, smelt — he loved them all. He and Dill had been fishing together since they were just out of diapers. He had the photo evidence to prove it.

"Let me ask the boss and I'll text you."

Willie nodded. He and Dill were quite proud of their texting skills these days. Not many of their retired friends had gotten on board with that particular method of communication, but Willie found that his nieces all stayed in touch more frequently if he texted them rather than called or emailed. No one wrote letters anymore since his wife, Velma, died.

Dill laid the chart down and leaned back against the counter in the small examination room at Loon Lake Hospital. "How's Cassie these days? I haven't seen her much."

Willie slid off the exam table and tucked his shirt into his trousers. "She's busy with her final papers and exams. Graduation's coming up in a month or so and she wants to have perfect scores. You know how she is."

Dill ran a hand through his snowy white hair. "Oh, yeah. Beth's the same."

Willie's youngest niece, Cassie, had been driving back and forth to Northwestern Michigan College in Traverse City, about forty miles away, often carpooling with Dill's granddaughter, Beth.

"How's Cassie doing with, uh, you know." Dill waved his hand vaguely through the air.

Willie shook his head. "Single and determined to stay that way, I guess. I wouldn't say that Fletcher fella broke her heart as much as he humiliated her. Makin' like you're gonna ask a woman to marry you, and then high-tailing it outta town soon as the grass gets greener...that's no kind of man for my Cassie."

"If this were the Wild West, we could chase after him with shotguns."

"If we're chasing after folks with shotguns, seems like we shoulda started with Danny. But that ship's sailed and I haven't been able to turn it around for anything."

Danny Kessler was like a son to Willie, just like Cassie was like a daughter. The two kids had grown up together in Loon Lake, had been all but joined at the hip since kindergarten. He'd thought for sure they'd wind up together. But just about the time the two of them had started noticing that their best friend was a little more interesting, a new girl had sailed into town and ruined everything. Danny had fallen hard for Bright Shiny, the not-so-secret nickname his friend Jax had given Lily.

"He still downstate doing construction?"

Willie nodded. "He's been working his way up in that big construction company near Lansing. Getting promoted, doing more than they ask, getting noticed." He didn't try to keep the pride out of his voice. He'd been the one to give Danny his first hammer.

"Maybe you should drop a hint that Cassie's available."

Willie snorted. "Oh, he knows. He pretends he doesn't care, but he's been asking about her more since I mentioned it a few months ago. But if I can't get the boy to come up and visit for anything but holidays, I don't see how I can get them together again. Too bad I'm not dying," he said as an afterthought. "That would put a fire under his behind for a visit."

Dill chuckled. "Yeah, well, we're all dying, aren't we?"

"Sooner or later," Willie agreed. Sooner or later...hmm. "You know," he said slowly, his brow furrowing in thought, "it wouldn't be a lie. You just said it yourself."

Dill took a step toward the door and held up his hands as if warding off Willie's words. He was used to Willie's crazy ideas after sixty-odd years of friendship, but he didn't like to hear them at first. "Hold on, where you going with this?"

Willie feigned an innocent expression. "I'm just repeating what my doctor told me. I'm dying. The kids should know so they can help me make my final plans. I'll need both of them to help get my affairs in order. Right?"

Willie waited and was soon rewarded. Dill grinned and dropped his hands to his hips. His friend couldn't resist the cockamamie plans they cooked up together.

"It just might work," Dill said.

"We can make our plans tonight on the lake. Bring a notebook."

Dill waggled his phone in the air. "We can use the notes app on our phones, remember?"

"Right, right," Willie agreed. The two men were determined to be the most tech-savvy senior citizens in Loon Lake. Willie walked to the door and slapped Dill on the shoulder. "This'll be fun. I've always liked Christmas weddings."

ALSO BY KITTY BUCHOLTZ

CONSIDER BUYING BOOKS DIRECT FROM KITTY! GO TO KITTYBUCHOLTZ.COM/BOOKS

The Strays of Loon Lake

Welcome to Loon Lake

Love at the Fluff and Fold

Traverse City in Love

Cherry on Top (free short story)

Little Miss Lovesick

Death and Tacos (coming soon!)

Adventures of Lewis and Clarke

Superhero in Disguise

A Very Merry Superhero Wedding

Unexpected Superhero

My Bullheaded Superhero Valentine

Also…

Adventures of Lewis and Clarke: The Beginning (the first three books)

A NOTE FROM KITTY

This story was originally published as *Rescue at Loon Lake* in the anthology *Moonlit Encounters*. When I finished writing it, I realized it was the start of a new romantic comedy series. And possibly the best thing about it — there would be a dog in every book! *Loon Lake, where stray dogs and lost men find a forever home.* Chip the border collie, as it turns out, is the father of Pirate, the puppy who appears in the next book, *Love at the Fluff and Fold.* Over time, characters from the Strays of Loon Lake series and the Traverse City in Love chick lit series will show up in each other's books!

If you enjoyed this book, check out my Adventures of Lewis and Clarke superhero urban fantasy series. The short story prequel, *Superhero in Disguise*, is the story of how Tori and Joe met on Halloween. *A Very Merry Superhero Wedding* is about their Christmas Eve wedding during a Christmastime crime spree. And *Unexpected Superhero* tells the story of what happens when Tori finds out why she's different. (You can read all three stories in the omnibus, *Adventures of Lewis and Clarke: The Beginning*.) Then their best friends, Bull and Hayley, finally go out on a real date in *My Bullheaded Superhero Valentine*.

My books are available as ebooks and in print at most online retailers. *Unexpected Superhero* and *Little Miss Lovesick* are also available as audiobooks. All the ebooks, print books, and audiobooks will be added to my own web store over the course of 2024. Purchases there support me and my work in a significantly greater way so I'd love it if you'd like to buy from me directly (kittybucholtz.com/books)!

You can also join my free or paid membership community over on Patreon (links at the end of About the Author). Read chapters early before the books even come out, discuss the stories with other readers, see fun art about the settings of the books, and more!

Would you like to read *Cherry on Top* for free? It's set in the same town as *Little Miss Lovesick* during the famous National Cherry Festival. It's my gift to you when you join my reader newsletter at kittybucholtz.com/freebook. Enjoy!

And if you really want to make my day, I'd love for you to post your thoughts about any of my books in a review. Thanks so much!

Just so you know, I rebranded all my books in 2024 to be "sweet" — so no swear words or overt sex scenes. I hope you enjoy the change.

Thanks for spending part of your day with me. I hope you have a great tomorrow!

Happy Reading!

ACKNOWLEDGMENTS

I've never written a (good) book by myself. I'm always grateful to everyone who is willing to help make my stories better.

Thank you to Diane Barney, Bonnie L. DePue OTR/L HPCS, Joel Dorr, Alan B. Douglass, Rick Ochocki, DeeAnn Visk, and Dr. Kate Wisser MD for helping me get the medical parts right. Any mistakes are all me.

Thank you for the story and editing support of my Sydney writers group, The Writers Coven — Ann, Bernadette, Coleen, Deb, Jen, Judy, Margie, Paula, and Shaz. I always worry I don't make a good team player, but putting an anthology together with you was more fun than I expected.

Thank you to my editor Marcy Weydemuller for your unflagging support, and Denise Colby for your excellent proofreading skills.

Thank you to Kathleen Wright for giving me a ton of advice about dogs and dog ownership, and for reading the final version and reassuring me that I got it right.

And last, but never least, thank you to my readers for telling me over and over to hurry and get this series out! You're the reason I'm so far behind in *Castle* re-runs. I love you guys!

ABOUT THE AUTHOR

Kitty Bucholtz writes sweet romantic comedy and superhero urban fantasy, often with an inspirational element woven in. Her stories feature women whose sense of humor and nervous gutsiness get them into and out of all kinds of trouble. She grew up forty miles east of Traverse City, Michigan—where she loves to set her books. She went to college there, met and married the love of her life, and waved goodbye to everything she knew when she and her husband, John, struck out for parts unknown.

Their romantic adventures have included a scolding at Parliament House in Belfast for canoodling, three trips Down Under where her handsome hubby made animated movie animals look real, and a delicious taste of European life living in Sweden. After earning her M.A. in Creative Writing in Sydney, she formed Daydreamer Entertainment and began self-publishing. Founder of Write Now! Workshop and Write Now! Workshop Podcast, she loves to teach and coach writers.

Only God knows where they'll wind up next – but they're pretty sure it will be another cool chapter in their adventure!

If you enjoyed this or any of Kitty's books, please leave a review—they are a tremendous help to both writers and readers!

Connect with Kitty today!

kittybucholtz.com
kitty@kittybucholtz.com

Get your copy of the free short story *Cherry on Top* at kittybucholtz.com/freebook today!

patreon.com/kittybucholtz

tiktok.com/@kitty_bucholtz

facebook.com/kittybucholtzauthor

bookbub.com/profile/kitty-bucholtz

amazon.com/author/kittybucholtz

x.com/KittyBucholtz

instagram.com/kittybucholtz

goodreads.com/kittybucholtz

youtube.com/kittybucholtz

www.ingramcontent.com/pod-product-compliance
Lightning Source LLC
Chambersburg PA
CBHW050912120626
46552CB00004B/1541